To Matt & Anne —

with love and best wishes
to your family!!

Deb Davis

à la famille

Did You Know?

written by Deb Davis

illustrated by Jean-Paul Jacquet

With thanks to our support team: Chris Atwood, Brad Davis, Josh Lake and Melissa Rowe.

ISBN: 9781619273443

for families everywhere

Did you know when Old Man Rooster crows,
And Jolly Mrs. Sun pops up and glows,

When warm and gentle breezes blow,
And the morning bursts with song...

That in a distant far-off place,
The man-in-the-moon with a polished face,

Whispers, "Good night, sweet dreams!" through space,
And the evening nods with a yawn?

Did you know as the city lights flash and flare,
And the horns of the yellow cabs blast and blare,

And the cars and the people rush who knows where,
And the clamor and movement don't stop...

That on a distant far-off hill,
A young girl walks so soft and still,

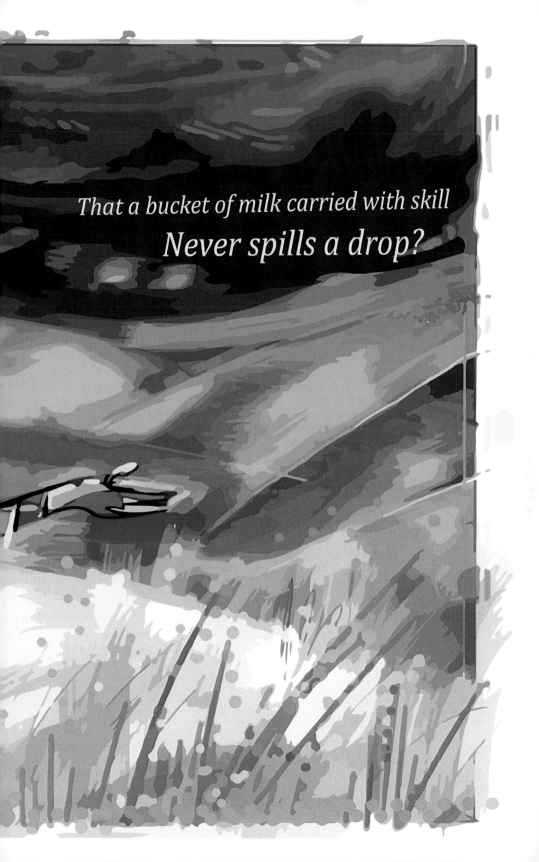

That a bucket of milk carried with skill
Never spills a drop?

Did you know as you climb in your car for a ride,
And down the road you smoothly glide,

That in a distant far-off spot,
A rider is bumping, all dusty and hot

As his camel is starting off at a trot
In search of something green?

Did you know as you jump and hop and run
And sweat and swim under blistering sun,

And the days grow long and so full of fun
That you leap and squeal with glee...

That in a distant far-off land,
Someone sculpting a snow palace grand

Shivers and shapes with mittened hand
A wonder that few will see?

Did you know as your Mom and Dad dim the light,
And they hug and kiss you and whisper, "Sleep tight,"

And you know that they love you with all their might,
And you feel the same way, too...

That on a distant far-off shore,
A Mom and a Dad just like yours

Are loving with hugs and kisses galore,

Someone just like you?